Presented to

_____

from

_____

_____

_____ 19____

Dear Parents:

Halloween is one of most young children's favorite celebrations during the year. It gives them an opportunity to dress up, pretend, and share the excitement of a special occasion with friends.

This book is a non-scary, rhyming story that is especially written for the very young child who may be discovering the celebration of Halloween for the first time. The simple activities at Barney's party are appropriate for the youngest preschooler.

We consider books to be lifelong gifts that develop and enhance the love of reading. We hope you enjoy reading along with Barney, Baby Bop and BJ!

Mary Ann Dudko, Ph.D.
Margie Larsen, M.Ed.
Early Childhood Education Specialists

Art Director: Tricia Legault
Designer: Darren McKee

Barney™

PUBLISHING

300 East Bethany Drive, Allen, Texas 75002

Printed at Color Dynamics, Allen, Texas 75002

5 6 7 8 9 10   00 99 98

ISBN 1-57064-046-7

Library of Congress Number 96-83766

Barney's Halloween Party

Written by Mary Ann Dudko and Margie Larsen

Illustrated by Darren McKee

Once a year on Halloween night
Pumpkins and scarecrows come into sight.

There are spiders and ghosts
To decorate the room.
Barney better hurry,
His friends are coming soon.

There's a knock at the door.
Who can it be?
A princess, a pirate,
Who else do you see?

There are pumpkins to carve
With bright shining faces.
Where should we put them?
We know many good places.

Let's stuff a scarecrow
And sit him up tall.

He wears a straw hat
And blue overalls.

Barney plays music
For a Halloween dance.
Look at the friends
As they skip, twirl, and prance.

A Halloween moon
Lights up the sky.
Let's trick or treat
At houses nearby.

We'll knock on the door
And shout "Trick or Treat!"
Now open your bags
For good things to eat.

We see monsters and ghosts
As we walk down the street.
What other friends
Do you think we will meet?

Our bags are now full,
And it's getting late.
Time to go home.
Trick or treating was great!

Halloween night
Is almost done.
So blow out the candles.
Barney hopes you had fun!

Happy Halloween!